STAN the ELEPHANT

MANICA K. MUSIL

HAVE EITHER OF
YOU SEEN STAN?

HE'S PROBABLY HARASSING
SOMEONE AGAIN WITH
HIS STORIES!

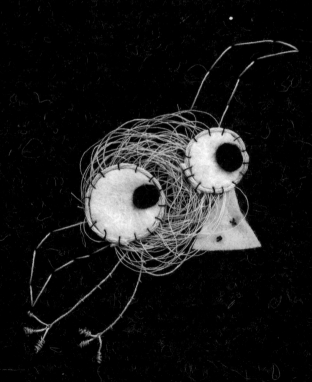

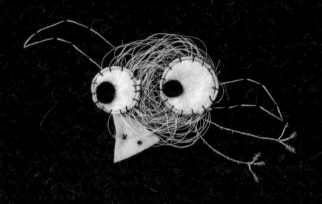

LET'S GO
FIND OUT!

Published in 2020 by Windmill Books,
an Imprint of Rosen Publishing
29 East 21st Street, New York, NY 10010

Translated from the Slovenian by Jason Blake

Cataloging-in-Publication Data
Names: Musil, Manica K.
Title: Stan the elephant / Manica K. Musil.
Description: New York : Windmill Books, 2020.
Identifiers: ISBN 9781725394025 (pbk.) | ISBN 9781725394049 (library bound) | ISBN 9781725394032 (6 pack)
Subjects: LCSH: Elephants--Juvenile fiction. | Storytelling--Juvenile fiction. | Friendship--Juvenile fiction.
Classification: LCC PZ7.M875 St 2020 | DDC [E]--dc23

Manufactured in the United States of America

CPSIA Compliance Information: Batch #BS19WM: For Further Information contact Rosen Publishing, New York, New York at 1-800-237-9932

Stan the Elephant

MANICA K. MUSIL

translated by Jason Blake

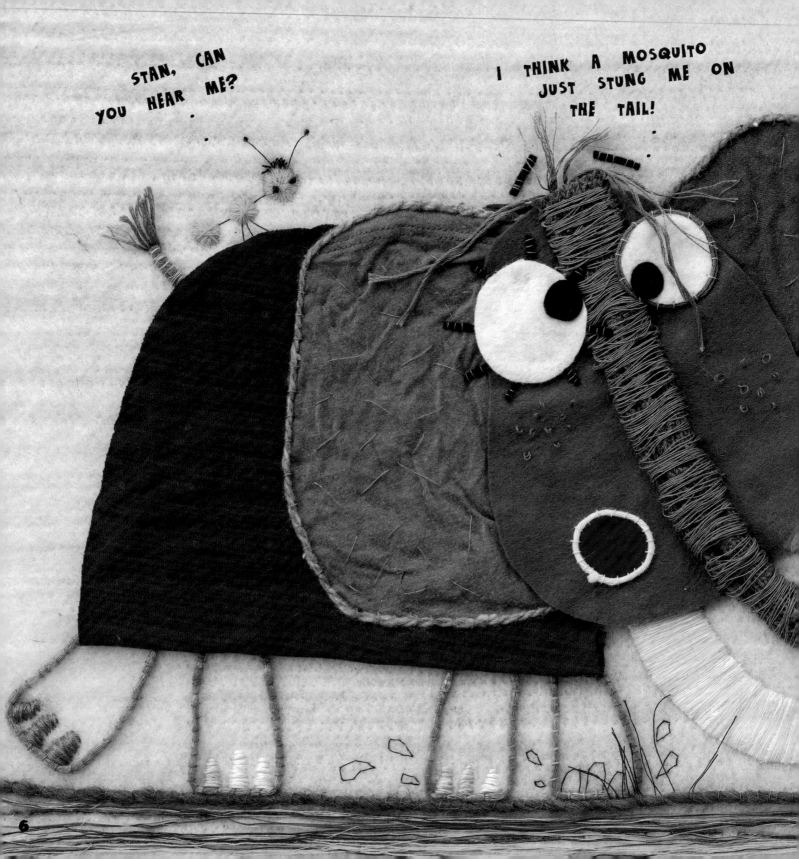

My name's **Stan**, and I just love telling **StorieS**.
But everyone says my stories are without rhyme or reason.

ONCE STAN STARTS
TELLING HIS TALES,
THE WORDS JUST POUR
RIGHT OUT OF HIM.

BUT HE'S NEVER
TOLD AN INTERESTING
TALE HIS
WHOLE LIFE.

Today, as usual, Stan set out to find a
listeNer for his Stories.

CAN I TELL YOU A STORY?

YOU DOPE, WHO WANTS TO TELL TALES TO A CROCODILE?

9

He went up to the **ZeBra**, who was grazing nearby.

WHY ARE YOU
RUNNING AWAY
FROM ME?

AH, STAN, YOU'VE
JUST STOMPED OVER
ALL OUR GRASS!

But before Stan could say hi, she was already fleeiNG.

I DON'T WANT
TO HEAR YOUR
YAPPING!

YOU REALLY
ARE A DOPEY
ELEPHANT.

He went up to the liON, who was stretching out in the Sun.
But before Stan could say hi, he already had to flee.

12

Not even the other elephants in Stan's herd wanted to listen to him.

BROTHERS, SISTERS,
SOMETHING REALLY INTERESTING
HAPPENED TO ME
TODAY ...

TELL ME!
FORGET ABOUT
YOUR HERD.

14

The **Parrots** had enough to talk about by themselves and had no time for Stan's **tales**.

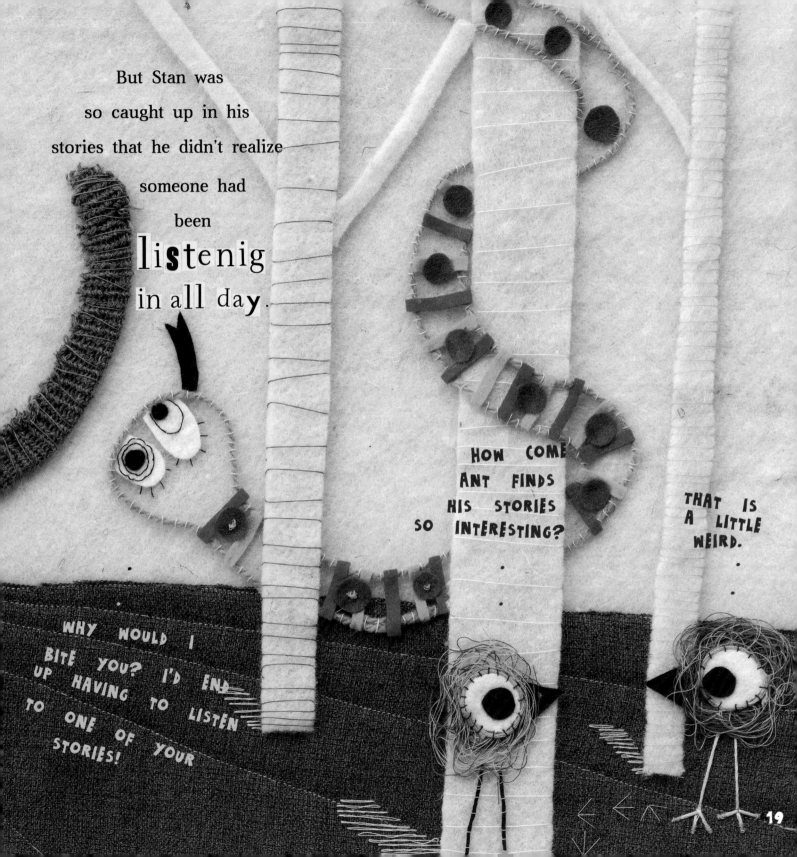

But Stan was so caught up in his stories that he didn't realize someone had been **listenig in all day**.

WHY WOULD I BITE YOU? I'D END UP HAVING TO LISTEN TO ONE OF YOUR STORIES!

HOW COME ANT FINDS HIS STORIES SO INTERESTING?

THAT IS A LITTLE WEIRD.

That afternoon, as Stan lay moping on a pile of leaves, the tiny little voiCe finally reached his earS.

WHAT CAN
YOU DO?
IT'S LOVE.

"Who are you?" asked Stan.

"I'd love you **to tell me a Story**," answered **ANt**.

"Well, why didn't you say so?" asked Stan.

WHAT A CUTE COUPLE ...

STOP BOUNCING ON MY HEAD!

"I told you a thousand times, but you did**N**'t he**a**r e**Ve**N o**NC**e!" moaned Ant.

"Can I tell you **oNe** now?" asked Stan, delighted.

WHERE ARE
WE GOING?

ONCE UPON A
TIME, BACK WHEN
I WAS A BAT...

DO WE REALLY
HAVE TO TRY
EVERYTHING OUT?

And **S**tan started to **tell** **tales** to **ANt**.
The two of them told each other stories all through the night and into the next day.

ARE THOSE
TWO BATTY?

HOW ABOUT IF
WE TICKLE
HIM?

Even though the zebras, crocodiles, lions, other elephants, snakes, and parrots still had no interest in Stan's stories, Stan was ha**PP**y as could be. He'd found someone to l**i**s**t**E**n** to him... and so what if it was just a little a**N**t?

REALLY?
AND THEN
WHAT HAPPENED?

HA, HA, HA.
WHAT A
MESS!

30

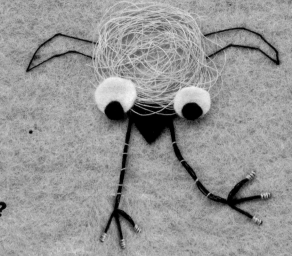

DOESN'T IT
SEEM BORING
WITHOUT STAN?

YES, LET'S GO
JOIN ANT.

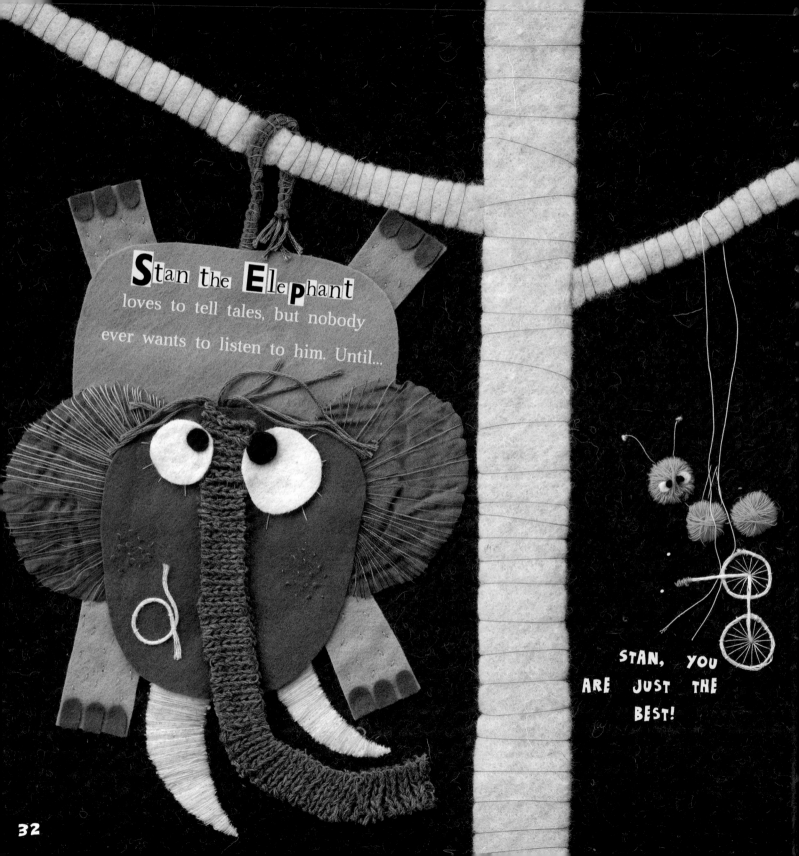

Stan the E**l**e**p**hant loves to tell tales, but nobody ever wants to listen to him. Until...

STAN, YOU ARE JUST THE BEST!